Go Mat!

Written by Clare Helen Welsh
Illustrated by Lucy Barnard

Collins

I pick a mat.

I pack the mat.

Kit sits on it.

Go mat! Go Kit!

Mack sits on it.

Go Kit! Go Mack!

Sock the cat sits.

The mat can go!

Mack! Mop the dots.

Kit! Pat Kim the dog.

I can sit on it.

The mat can go!

13

/c/

14

ck

15

 After reading

Letters and Sounds: Phase 2

Word count: 50

Focus phonemes: /g/ /o/ /c/ /k/ ck

Common exception words: the, I, go

Curriculum links: Personal, social and emotional development

Early learning goals: Reading: read and understand simple sentences; use phonic knowledge to decode regular words and read them aloud accurately; read some irregular words

Developing fluency

- Your child may enjoy hearing you read the book.
- Take turns to read a page, demonstrating how to read with expression. Encourage your child to read the sentences ending in exclamation marks with extra emphasis and excitement.

Phonic practice

- Turn to pages 10–11. Point to **Kit** on page 11. Ask your child to sound out the letter in each word, then blend. (K/i/t – **Kit**) Can your child find a word with the same /k/ sound but spelled with two letters and not just one? (*Mack*)
- Take turns to point out a word for each other to sound out and blend. Sound a letter out incorrectly once or twice, saying: Have I got that right? Encourage your child to correct you.
- Look at the "I spy sounds" pages (14–15). Point to the /c/ and "ck" at the corners of the pages and sound them out. Say: I can see lots of things that have the /c/ sound. Point to the caravan and say: caravan, emphasising the /c/ sound. Repeat for the picture, emphasising the /c/ in the middle. Ask your child to find more things that contain the /c/ sound. (*clock, cup, cushion, car, cake, Sock, camel, bricks, cupboard*) Talk about the "ck" spelling in clock, Sock and bricks.

Extending vocabulary

- Look at each double page in turn and take turns to point to a character and ask: Who is it? Explore the relationships, asking: What is Mack's sister doing? What is Kit's brother doing?